JUST ME AND MY DAD

BY MERCER MAYER

A GOLDEN BOOK
NEW YORK

Golden Books Publishing Company, Inc.,
New York, New York 10106

A GOLDEN BOOK • NEW YORK

Golden Books Publishing Company, Inc., New York, New York 10106

Just Me and Dad book, characters, text, and images © 1975 Mercer Mayer. LITTLE CRITTER, MERCER MAYER'S LITTLE CRITTER, and MERCER MAYER'S LITTLE CRITTER Logo are registered trademarks of Orchard House Licensing Company. All rights reserved. Printed in the U.S.A. No part of this book may be reproduced or copied in any form without written permission from the copyright owner. GOLDEN BOOKS®, A GOLDEN BOOK®, G DESIGN®, and the distinctive spine are registered trademarks of Golden Books Publishing Company, Inc. A GOLDEN STORYBOOK™ is a trademark of Golden Books Publishing Company, Inc. Library of Congress Catalog Card Number: 77-73591   11 10 9 8 7 6   ISBN: 0-307-11839-8   MM

We went camping,
just me and my dad.
Dad drove the car
because I'm too little.

I picked the campsite, but someone
was already living there.
So I gave it back.

We found another
campsite nearby.
My dad was tired,
so I pitched the tent.

We made a campfire.
I found the wood,
and my dad lit the fire.

I wanted to take my dad
for a ride in our canoe,
but I launched it too hard.

We went fishing instead.

My dad took a snapshot
of the fish we caught.
Then I cooked dinner
for me and my dad.

We had eggs.

After dinner, I told my dad a ghost story.
Boy, did he get scared!

I gave my dad a big hug.
That made him feel better.

Then we went to bed.

I stayed up with my dad and let him read a story to me.

We slept in our tent all night long—
just me and my dad.